Connecting Cultures Through Family and Food

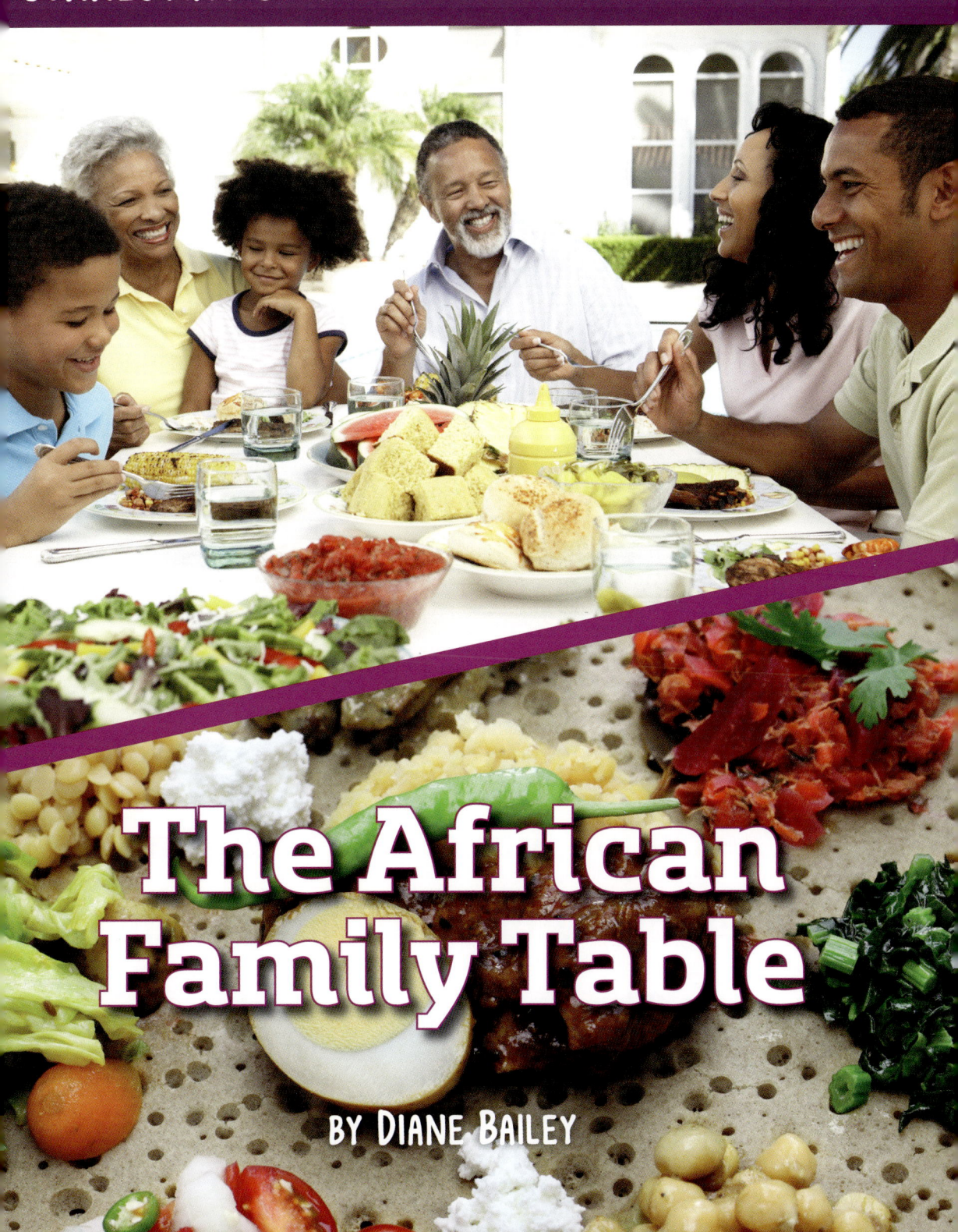

The African Family Table

by Diane Bailey

Connecting Cultures Through Family and Food

The African Family Table

The Chinese Family Table

The Greek Family Table

The Indian Family Table

The Italian Family Table

The Japanese Family Table

The Mexican Family Table

The Middle Eastern Family Table

The Native American Family Table

The South American Family Table

The Thai Family Table

CONNECTING CULTURES THROUGH FAMILY AND FOOD

The African Family Table

By Diane Bailey

MASON CREST

Mason Crest
450 Parkway Drive, Suite D
Broomall, PA 19008
www.masoncrest.com

© 2019 by Mason Crest, an imprint of National Highlights, Inc.

All rights reserved. No part of this publication may be reproduced or transmitted in any form or by any means, electronic or mechanical, including photocopying, recording, taping, or any information storage and retrieval system, without permission in writing from the publisher.

Printed and bound in the United States of America.

First printing
9 8 7 6 5 4 3 2 1

Series ISBN: 978-1-4222-4041-0
Hardback ISBN: 978-1-4222-4042-7
EBook ISBN: 978-1-4222-7740-9

Produced by Shoreline Publishing Group LLC
Santa Barbara, California
Editorial Director: James Buckley Jr.
Designer: Tom Carling
Production: Patty Kelley
www.shorelinepublishing.com
Front cover: MBI/Shutterstock.com

Library of Congress Cataloging-in-Publication Data
Names: Bailey, Diane, 1966- author. Title: The African family table / by Diane Bailey. Other titles: Connecting cultures through family and food.
Description: Broomall, PA : Mason Crest, 2018. | Series: Connecting cultures through family and food | Includes index.
Identifiers: LCCN 2017053409| ISBN 9781422240427 (hardback) | ISBN 1422240428 (hardback) | ISBN 9781422277409 (ebook)
Subjects: LCSH: Cooking, African--Juvenile literature. | Africans--Food--Juvenile literature. | Africans--Social life and customs--Juvenile literature.
Classification: LCC TX725.A35 B35 2018 | DDC 641.59/296073--dc23 LC record available at https://lccn.loc.gov/2017053409

QR Codes disclaimer:

You may gain access to certain third party content ("Third-Party Sites") by scanning and using the QR Codes that appear in this publication (the "QR Codes"). We do not operate or control in any respect any information, products, or services on such Third-Party Sites linked to by us via the QR Codes included in this publication, and we assume no responsibility for any materials you may access using the QR Codes. Your use of the QR Codes may be subject to terms, limitations, or restrictions set forth in the applicable terms of use or otherwise established by the owners of the Third-Party Sites. Our linking to such Third-Party Sites via the QR Codes does not imply an endorsement or sponsorship of such Third-Party Sites, or the information, products, or services offered on or through the Third- Party Sites, nor does it imply an endorsement or sponsorship of this publication by the owners of such Third-Party Sites.

Contents

Introduction 6

1. Getting Here 8
APPETIZER 20
2. Settling In 22
MAIN COURSE 32
3. Connecting 34
SECOND COURSE 44
4. Reaching Back 48
DESSERT 58

Find Out More 62

Series Glossary of Key Terms 63

Index/Author 64

KEY ICONS TO LOOK FOR

Words to Understand: These words with their easy-to-understand definitions will increase the reader's understanding of the text, while building vocabulary skills.

Sidebars: This boxed material within the main text allows readers to build knowledge, gain insights, explore possibilities, and broaden their perspectives by weaving together additional information to provide realistic and holistic perspectives.

Educational Videos: Readers can view videos by scanning our QR codes, providing them with additional educational content to supplement the text. Examples include news coverage, moments in history, speeches, iconic moments, and much more!

Text-Dependent Questions: These questions send the reader back to the text for more careful attention to the evidence presented here.

Research Projects: Readers are pointed toward areas of further inquiry connected to each chapter. Suggestions are provided for projects that encourage deeper research and analysis.

Series Glossary of Key Terms: This back-of-the-book glossary contains terminology used throughout this series. Words found here increase the reader's ability to read and comprehend higher-level books and articles in this field.

Introduction

The story of all people begins in Africa. The earliest ancestors of humans lived on the continent several million years ago. And about 200,000 years ago, the first *homo sapiens*—modern humans—evolved there. At almost 12 million square miles (31 million sq km), it's an enormous continent that straddles the equator. Dense, dripping rain forests clustered in the center of the continent give way to the vast, dry expanses of sand of the Sahara Desert in the north. People live in a Mediterranean climate on the north coast and in semi-arid and temperate regions in the south. That geographical diversity has helped produce a huge amount of physical and cultural diversity, as well.

Tens of thousands of years ago, people began migrating throughout Africa. Eventually, about 60,000 years ago, they moved into Europe, Asia, and eventually the Americas. Sometimes these migrations were voluntary. At other times, especially from the 1600s through the 1800s, they were not, as millions of African natives were shipped to other parts of the world and sold as slaves.

Whatever the reasons or circumstances for their movement, as Africans spread into different parts of the world, they left their mark in numerous ways. Styles of music and dance that grew out of traditional African culture, such as jazz and hip-hop, are now part of mainstream society. And all over the world, modern ways of eating have their roots in Africa. Gumbo from the Caribbean,

Introduction 7

pan-fried cornbread from the southern United States, and the couscous craze in France can all trace their history to Africa.

Today, with more than 50 countries, Africa is a fascinating blend of diversity and unity. Its individual nations, and the regions they belong to, each have distinct cultures, but they are tied together by a shared history. Whatever their differences, they are all still African.

Getting Here

It might be one of history's most notable "food fights." Sometime around the 14th century, two sons of an African king got into a fight with their father over palm wine. Was it about how to make it? (Hint: Start with the sap of a flavorful palm tree, like a coconut.) Was it over who deserved to receive a few bottles as a gift? Was it about who had, um, a bit too much?

The details of this dust-up are fuzzy, but it didn't end well. Fed up with his sons, the king disinherited them both and selected his daughter to take over after he died.

Words to Understand

commodities raw materials or agricultural products that are bought and sold

economic depressions periods of time in which the economy of a country or a region declines and money is worth less; wages fall and work is harder to find

exploiting taking unfair advantage of

infrastructure the basic organizational and physical (such as roads and power plants) structures needed to run a society

restrictive presenting difficulties or limitations

Africa has a long history of kingdoms, countries, and tribes. The rich tradition of African art is popular among 21st-century collectors.

Which didn't take long—his sons killed him.

Meanwhile, a couple of kingdoms over, another young man was denied his father's throne. The king accused his son of being cowardly, although in truth he was just jealous of his son's hunting skills. Realizing he had no future at home, the son set out for distant lands. He met the daughter of the other king (now in charge of her father's land), married her, and went on to establish his own powerful kingdom. In doing so, Chibinda Ilunga became one of Africa's most famous immigrants, writing his name into history.

The Slave Trade

Before the year 1500, people all over Africa were migrants. Some, like Chibinda Ilunga, moved within the continent. Others crossed into Europe and Asia. Some were chasing power or wealth, but most were likely just seeking a modest version of a better life.

Unfortunately, much of the history of Africa has a sadder story. As people from other countries began exploring—and **exploiting**—the resources of Africa, humans became one of the top **commodities**. People were captured to be sold into slavery. They were rounded up and put in chains and pens. Some slaves were shipped north, to areas such as Portugal or the Netherlands. Others went to the Middle East, India, and Asia.

The best-known story of African slavery, however, is the trans-Atlantic trade that brought slaves to the Americas. In a complex pattern known as the "triangle trade," the Europeans brought goods south to Africa, where they sold them and used the money to buy slaves. During the second part of the cycle, the "middle passage," slaves were shipped to the Americas, first to South and Central America and later to the United States. There,

The horrible stain of slavery remains an unresolved issue in relations between many African Americans and white Americans.

the slaves were sold so Europeans could buy raw materials such as sugar and cotton. They carried that cargo back to Europe, where it was processed into manufactured goods. Then the horrible cycle began again.

The slave trade flourished for more than three centuries, from the early 1500s to the mid-1800s. During that time, it's estimated that more than 12 million Africans, mostly from the western and central parts of the continent, were forcibly taken from their homes. Some two million of them died during the journey, while the remaining ones went into unpaid forced labor, mining silver in Peru, raising coffee in Brazil, growing sugar in the Caribbean, and tending rice, cotton, and tobacco in the southern United States. Most lived lives of great poverty, stress, and danger.

A New Era

In the United States, the extended brutality of slavery eventually resulted in a violent conflict: the Civil War. After this bloody war ended in 1865, slavery was abolished, although it took another century for conditions for African Americans to substantially improve. Many white people, especially in the South, still thought of blacks as inferior. Blacks had nowhere

After the Civil War ended, African Americans still faced poverty, discrimination, and want, even as they worked to "rise up."

The Middle Passage

The captains of ships that carried slaves to the New World did not care whether their passengers were comfortable. Slaves were kept in miserable conditions, crammed body-to-body in tiny spaces. They often did not have enough room to sit up, or have a place to go to the bathroom. But the captains did have to keep their cargo alive, and healthy enough that they could be sold for a profit. That meant they had to feed them—and what's more, they had to feed them something they would actually eat. Ship captains stocked corn for slaves who came from present-day Angola; rice for those from the areas of Senegal and The Gambia; and yams for slaves taken from modern Nigeria. Traders also noted that slaves had a "good stomach for beans." A few lemons or limes were added to prevent scurvy, and occasionally some fish caught during the journey. The traders' strategy did not always work. Captives often went on hunger strikes during the voyage, preferring to die rather than enter a life of slavery.

near the same opportunities, rights, and freedoms as whites enjoyed. Not surprisingly, only a small number of native Africans immigrated to the United States during the century after the end of the Civil War, and most of those were white people from South Africa.

By the 1960s, though, the world was changing. Up through the first half of the 20th century, many countries in Africa were under colonial rule, meaning they were controlled by the governments of other nations, notably Britain and France. As colonial rule weakened, these nations gained their independence. However, many of them were not prepared for self-rule. They did not have the institutions or **infrastructure** to manage the challenges of government. Civil wars broke out. Poverty and violence wracked the continent.

Many people were looking for a way out, but they also still had strong ties to the countries that had governed them for so long. For example, Algeria, a country in North Africa, was colonized by France in the 1830s and remained that way until the 1960s. Algerian immigrants began moving to France around World War I, when the country needed laborers to help in the war effort. Another wave of immigration came in the 1960s. Despite no longer being officially tied to France, many Algerians decided to draw on their shared history and language with France, and begin new lives there.

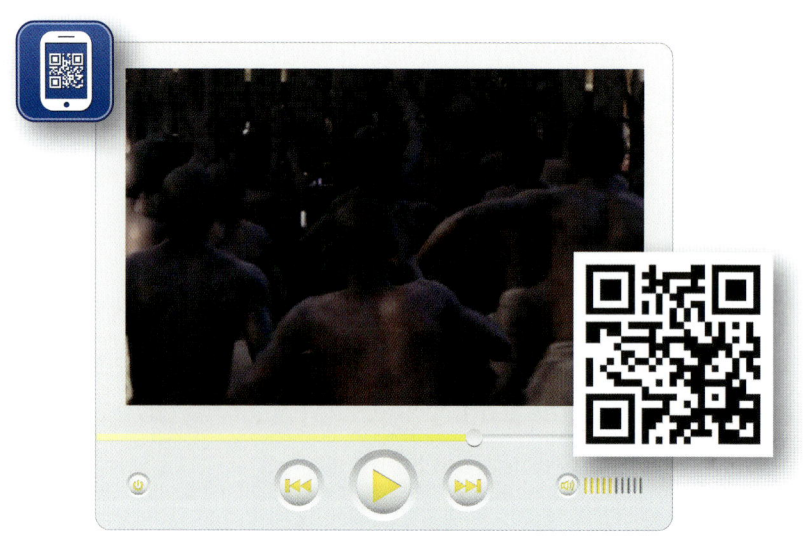

The Triangle Trade documentary

Land of Opportunity

The United States was another prime destination, especially because the mid-century upheaval in Africa coincided with major changes in America. In 1964, the U.S. passed a historic set of laws, the Civil Rights Act. It guaranteed equal rights to black people in everything from jobs to housing. Of course, deep-seated prejudices meant this didn't always happen in reality, but it was progress. The next year, **restrictive** immigration laws were loosened, making it easier for immigrants to enter the United States. The new policies encouraged students and skilled workers to come to America. It also allowed relatives of immigrants who were already here to join their families. Instead of a quota of a few hundred people per

Civil rights leader Dr. Martin Luther King Jr. watched as President Lyndon Johnson signed the Civil Rights Act of 1964.

country, now thousands were allowed in. Fifteen years later, in 1980, the US Refugee Act also made it easier for people in war-torn areas to come to America.

Akinde Kodjo-Sanogo immigrated to the United States from Côte D'Ivoire in 1995, to join her husband. "I immigrated here to have a better life, and fulfill my dreams, the American dream," she says. Between the language barrier (people in Côte D'Ivoire speak French), the high cost of living in New York, and a grueling work schedule, Kodjo-Sanogo says, "It was a difficult transition. I wanted to return to Africa because I did not like my

Parlez-Vous Français?

In the small city of Lewiston, Maine, about 15 percent of the population speaks French. That's because a lot of them are descendants of immigrants from French-speaking areas of Canada. Of course, English is Lewiston's primary language, but some of these second-generation immigrants meet regularly to eat lunch and converse in French. Most of them are older people who grew up with French-speaking parents from Canada, but take a look around the table and there are some new faces, too: African immigrants eager to communicate in French, their native tongue. There are few French speakers in the United States, so the language barrier can be a challenge. In Lewiston, Africans are grateful for translators who can guide them through the ins and outs of English, and the French-Canadians get a chance to keep their linguistic heritage alive—and help their fellow residents at the same time.

new life where you cannot visit friends. All you did was go to work, and come back home."

After more than 20 years, though, she's made adjustments that help her stay connected to her homeland. At monthly meetings with other immigrants, everyone brings a dish from their hometown to share. "The food makes us think about our home country," says Kodjo-Sanogo. "The way we eat together as one family, it creates love among us even though we come from different countries in Africa."

In recent years, immigration to the United States and Europe from Africa has risen, as families seek new opportunities in new lands.

Modern Migrations

Since the 1980s, migration from Africa has picked up markedly. Immigrants to the United States from countries in sub-Saharan Africa doubled each decade from the 1980s to the 2000s. European nations are other prime destinations, with Britain, France, Germany, and Italy drawing large numbers of immigrants. These are voluntary migrations in the sense that migrants have not been captured and enslaved. However, many would argue that their migration has been forced by circumstances. Political upheaval, environmental crises, and **economic depressions** have spurred many Africans to seek better lives elsewhere.

Fortunately, that's just one part of the picture, and not all immigrants are desperate. Over the past century, conditions in Africa have steadily improved in many parts of the continent. The stereotypical image of an uneducated, poverty-stricken family living off the land is only one slice of the African population. Many Africans live in cities and are skilled workers. It's those people, especially younger ones, who are leaving in the greatest numbers, looking for better job opportunities.

Thin injera bread is often served rolled up to be dipped in peanut sauce.

Even as African migrants leave their homes, they take with them the symbols of their rich culture, from their colorful traditional dress to their expressive music and dance. Perhaps nothing is more basic to a culture than its food. Over a bowl of *fufu* and lamb stew, or a piece of sour injera bread dipped in peanut sauce, sharing a meal has enabled Africans to hold their culture close even as they spread it throughout the world.

Text-Dependent Questions:

1. What was the route of the "triangle trade" that brought slaves to the Americas?

2. What two countries had the greatest presence in colonial Africa?

3. What is one reason that African immigrants in today's world are leaving their home countries?

Research Project:

Choose a country in Africa and research the immigrants who have come from there in recent years. What were some of the reasons they left? Where did they settle?

APPETIZER

Three meals a day is the standard eating schedule in the United States and other Western countries, but let's be realistic: Almost everyone sneaks some snacks in between, at least on occasion. The African way of eating is a little different. In most places, it's common for people to eat only two main meals, usually at midday and then again in the evening. Everyone gets the between-meals munchies sometimes, though, and Africans have a variety of snacks to calm their growling stomachs.

> *You don't need to go to a ball game for an excuse to eat peanuts—also called groundnuts—in African cuisine. Peanut oil and ground peanuts are used as flavorings in soups and stews, but they're also a quick, protein-packed pick-me-up for any time. Sometimes peanuts are roasted in sand to give them a distinctive flavor (the sand is removed before eating).*

Appetizer   21

Fritters are another popular snack throughout Africa. They start with a starchy fruit or vegetable, such as yams, peas, cassava, rice, maize, plantains, or any number of other fruits and vegetables. Try accara, *onion and garlic mixed with mashed black-eyed peas for a savory fritter, or dress up pumpkin with cinnamon, nutmeg, and sugar for a sweet one. Make a batter with flour and eggs, and then deep fry the whole thing. Fritters are easily adapted to whatever the cook has on hand. No yams? Substitute sweet potatoes. Maize can be replaced with corn. If you can't find plantains, bananas are fine. This versatility makes fritters a great way for African immigrants to cook the foods they ate at home while using ingredients that are available in their adopted country.*

2

Settling In

Imagine the American South before the Civil War. A powerful white man owns a plantation that grows cotton, rice, or tobacco. He has gotten rich off the work of the slaves he owns. His sons are able to follow in his footsteps and go into business; his wife and daughters occupy themselves with a steady stream of social activities. The responsibility to keep the house running smoothly falls to the lady of the house—but she doesn't do the work herself. It's the slaves who clean, do the laundry,

Words to Understand

cuisine a style or method of cooking in a particular culture

fusion in cooking, a blending of different regional styles to create a new style

networking using personal and business connections to advance in a career and life

palate the roof of the mouth, but also a person's taste for and understanding of different foods

renaissance a rebirth or period of growth; the term was first used to describe changes in some countries in Europe in the 1600s

22

Cotton was king among Southern plantation crops, but the only way it worked economically was that owners didn't pay for labor—they used slaves.

watch the young children, and tend the kitchen garden.

And of course, they cook, often to positive reactions from their white masters. After being served supper at a plantation, one Georgia diner noted, "If there is any one thing for which the African female intellect has a natural genius, it is for cooking." The racist nature of that statement does not take away from the excellence of the **cuisine**.

The Start of a New Cuisine

Cooking may not have been the most glamorous work, but there's no question this task gave black slaves some control over what went onto the dining room table. Maybe it was cornbread punched up with jalapeño peppers, or a jambalaya stew served over rice—both of which would have

Fried cornbread with jalapeño slices makes for a spicy breakfast treat.

been similar to what native Africans were eating. Served up on the fancy china, the food prepared by slave cooks was a kind of **fusion** cooking that drew on elements of both Africa and the Americas. It shaped the **palates** of their masters, and eventually would help to define tastes throughout the Caribbean and the American South.

What the slaves themselves ate differed dramatically from the luxurious meals of their white masters. Although some slaves were allowed to keep their own chickens and pigs, many had to rely on their owners for all their food. The white families had first choice of the desirable parts

What's Mine Is Yours

In Senegal, the Wolof people say *teranga*. The Mandinka in Mali use the term *diarama*. In South Africa, it's called *ubuntu*. Loosely translated, the words mean "hospitality." On the most basic level, an African's sense of hospitality requires them to offer a guest a glass of pineapple juice or a comfortable place to rest. But there's more to it. Pierre Thiam, a chef from Senegal, said in a 2015 interview with the radio show "The Splendid Table," "It's the way you treat the other, the one who is not you. ... There's always room for the other around your bowl. Why? Because we believe that the other is bringing blessings. When you share your bowl, your bowl will always be plentiful." As African immigrants begin to spread all over the world, they offered hospitality not only to people from their own nations, but to Africans in general—and to their adopted compatriots.

The savory dish of keshi yená *comes from the Caribbean island of Curaçao.*

of an animal—the chicken breasts, the pork ribs, the beef steaks. Slaves got the feet, the tails, or the intestines. From that, though, came dishes that are now Southern classics, such as chitterlings, which are the fried small intestines of pigs.

In the Caribbean and Brazil, okra, peppers, and palm oil were staples from Africa that began to show up in dishes that also featured New World crops such as bananas and mangoes. On the island of Curaçao, *keshi yená* features fish or meat cooked inside a cheese rind. The dish began with waste: Dutch slave owners would scoop out the creamy center of a rind of edam or gouda cheese, then throw the rind away—or rather, give it to the slaves to throw out. But the slaves, experts at stretching the little bit of food they got, rescued the rinds, stuffed them with fish, and then cooked them into a meal.

From Slave Food to Soul Food

African American slaves were granted their freedom after the Civil War, but for decades they were still treated as inferior. Throughout the South, they could not use the same bathrooms as whites, stay at the same hotels, or ride in the same sections on trains or buses. They weren't allowed to live in the same neighborhoods, and were often turned down for good jobs, even if they were qualified.

But there was one area that whites had little control over, and that was in the vibrant culture developing in black America. Blacks began to celebrate their African heritage and to draw on it to create original music, art, and dance styles. This movement was at its peak in New York during the 1920s, a period known as the Harlem **Renaissance**.

Cookbooks

To look at the titles of early US cookbooks, it's clear who was expected to do the cooking—as well as where some of the recipes came from. White housewives were the audience for Mary Randolph's *The Virginia House-wife*, published in 1824, but the cookbook also included recipes for things like okra soup and gumbo, which traced their origins to African cooking and the slave influence. Fifteen years later, another cookbook, *The Kentucky Housewife*, brought okra soup again to the pages, as well as recipes for stewed eggplant and pickles made from watermelon rinds. A few years after that, *The Carolina Housewife* included numerous recipes featuring rice, with which African American cooks had a lot of experience. In 1885, Lafcadio Hearn must have worked up an appetite after devising the title *La Cuisine Creole: A Collection of Culinary Recipes from Leading Chefs and Noted Creole Housewives, Who Have Made New Orleans Famous for Its Cuisine*. Happily, the recipes themselves were more straightforward. "Okra alone is vegetable enough for a gombo [sic]," he declared.

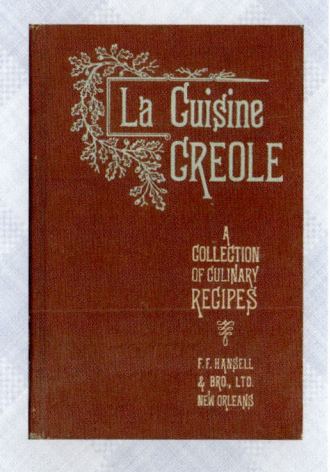

As the fight for civil rights intensified in the 1950s, African Americans refused to feel like second-class citizens—even when they were regularly treated that way. Black pride was growing, and with it came a desire to reconnect with their roots. Southern food, which had grown out of African traditions for centuries, became "soul food." On the plate, soul food could mean fried chicken smothered in gravy, a stew made with pigs' feet, collard greens flavored with pork fat, candied yams, and cornbread. For African Americans, soul food nourished more than their bodies; it fed their souls. It affirmed that their culture survived.

Creating Communities

After slavery was abolished, first in Europe and later in the Americas, the nature of African immigration changed. By the 1900s migrants were leaving their home countries voluntarily, although that did not translate to a new life without challenges or setbacks. Immigrants from all groups frequently faced discrimination from people in their adopted countries.

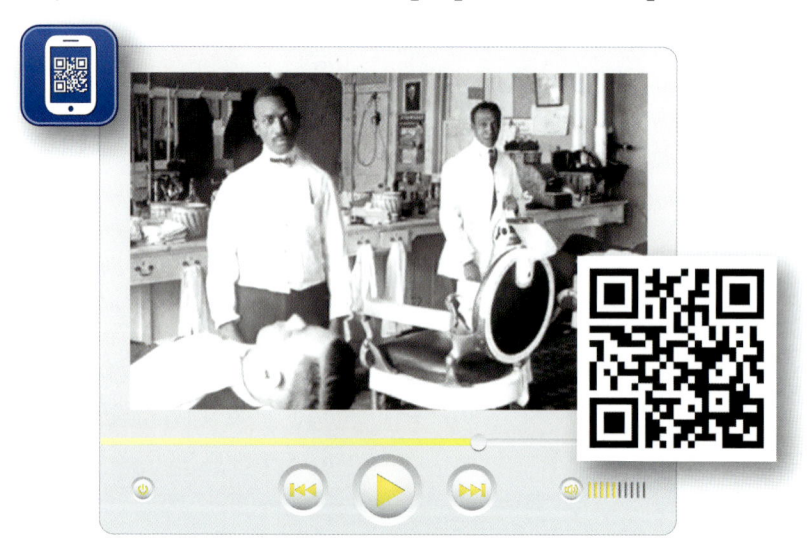

African Americans in the early 1900s

They might be labeled as lazy, criminal, stupid, or just strange. There wasn't much common ground, and native citizens often didn't want to share what ground there was. Africans faced particular challenges due to their darker skin, as well as lifestyles that could be vastly different from those in Asia or Western countries.

Their clothes and music were different, and much of their food was unfamiliar—not to mention their ways of eating it.

In Colorado Springs, an African American genealogical society helps people find ancestors.

For example, the African family "table" is sometimes just the floor, which is big enough to accommodate however many people show up.

Certainly, the citizens of some host countries were welcoming rather than suspicious, but African immigrants still struggled with language, economic, and cultural barriers. Naturally, they tended to seek each other out for support. Mel Tewahade, a businessman who lives in Denver, Colorado, emigrated from Ethiopia in the 1980s with just $20. Now, it's important to him to help new immigrants. "I help people in the community to get acclimated to American way of life and adjusting to cultural

A typical meal at an Ethiopian restaurant in Chicago.

differences," Tewahade said in a 2017 interview with the *Denver Post*. "Making life easier for newcomers."

Networking is a powerful tool, and new immigrants relied on more established ones for recommendations about where they could find a bed for the night, or who might have a lead on a job. Without established families or homes, they also flocked to restaurants that served their native food, finding comfort in both the cuisine and the company. These restaurants were part home kitchen, and part social hangout, a place to meet and connect with other immigrants.

At one Sudanese restaurant in Tel Aviv, Israel, there's no menu, but there doesn't need to be. Instead, the owner serves almost the same dishes every day. There might be *kabab hal*, a kind of meat stew; *bamya*, a stew made with okra and dill; or *asida*, a bread served with meat sauces. The style is ultra-casual. Customers aren't greeted by a host or served by a waiter; to order, they simply walk back to the kitchen, check out what's cooking on the stove, and pick out what they'd like.

The décor at the restaurant is laid-back, but notably, there are five televisions. One broadcasts a Sudanese channel, another has a station from Eritrea (a smaller country to the east of Sudan, which has also sent many immigrants to Israel), and one is Israeli. There's also a TV dedicated to the World Wrestling Federation, and yet another that plays movies. "For everyone," explains the owner. Anyone—everyone—is welcome here.

Text-Dependent Questions:

1. How was the dish *keshi yená* invented?
2. What was the Harlem Renaissance?
3. How do customers at the Sudanese restaurant in Tel Aviv place their orders?

Research Project:

Research some foods that are native to Africa. Which of them do you recognize and which are unfamiliar? Choose one food or spice and find out how it's now used in cuisines in other parts of the world.

MAIN COURSE

It's common in Western countries to serve meals in courses, but African cuisine thrives on being able to blend many tastes and textures into one big meal. A main dish of meat, fish, and vegetables is almost always accompanied by a starch, such as *injera*, a sour bread in Ethiopia, or *fufu*, which is traditionally made with pounded yams, but can be adapted to be made with flour from potatoes or other vegetables.

African cooks aren't shy about being generous with their seasonings, adding the heat of chili peppers or the bite of cumin to the main dish. The starchy sides aren't bland, but they're much milder, making them good partners to the main dish. Plus, there's no need to worry if there aren't any clean forks in the drawer: It's common to use the starch as a utensil. For example, diners can use a piece of bread or a pancake to scoop up bites of stew, or take a handful of fufu (pictured), roll it into a ball, and then dip it into their bowl.

Main Course 33

Fresh food is the way to go in Africa, and people routinely eat salads using fruit and vegetables from their gardens. A salad such as kachumbari combines tomatoes and onions with traditional African spices of chili peppers and coriander. Other salads focus on the tops of leafy greens like mustard, collards, turnips, and beets.

Water is the most common drink at an African meal, but for a treat, Africans might have a glass of oumo, or ginger beer. It's called "beer," but there's no alcohol. Instead, it blends grated ginger with pineapples, lemon juice, and sugar. And for a pick-me-up, nothing beats coffee, which is native to eastern Africa.

3

Connecting

You might love stocking up on your favorite foods at the grocery store or dread the trip up and down the aisles, but either way, it's probably not something you find especially difficult. That's not always the case for newly arrived African immigrants. For them, it can be one of the most baffling tasks in their new lives.

In Africa, it's common to buy food every day, at open-air markets, from vendors selling produce that was picked that morning from their gardens. But in Western countries, especially outside of major cities, the vast supermarket reigns supreme. Sure, it's filled with thousands of different items, but that's part of the problem—many African immigrants have no idea what those things are or how to eat them.

Words to Understand

mortar and pestle a kitchen tool for grinding hard foods into powder; the mortar is a small bowl, while the pestle is a rod or round-ended small club

plantain a fruit much like a banana, but starchier

simmer cook slowly over a low heat

taboo something that is forbidden by tradition

In Africa, many people depend on daily markets to find fresh produce, such as at this outdoor stand in a town in Kenya.

Wesley Tiku, a New Hampshire resident who moved from the West African country of Cameroon, remembers the confusion he felt during one of his first shopping trips. "Spinach was the thing that was most recognizable," he said in a 2014 interview with New Hampshire Public Radio.

Food can also be expensive. Living in New York, Akinde Kodjo-Sanogo did not have trouble finding African food—it was paying their high prices that created problems. To manage her budget, "I was eating more rice than anything, and I do not like rice!" she says.

Africans living outside of Africa bring their food traditions with them, such as this food stand at a market in Edinburgh, Scotland.

A Taste of Home

Tiku turned his confusing experience shopping into a business. He found a partner—an immigrant from Nepal—and together they opened a grocery that sells staples from Asia and Africa, including things like cassava, **plantain**, guava, and mustard greens. In fact, local markets catering to African customers have popped up all over the United States.

Vendors who sell their wares at the farmers' market in Minneapolis, Minnesota, have taken to growing African foods such as habañero peppers, kittley (a small eggplant, about the size of a grape, used for medicinal purposes), and bitter balls (an oval-shaped white eggplant nicknamed the garden egg).

Customers are eating it up. Blama Kollie and his wife, Makavee, drove eight hours from their North Dakota home to buy $500 worth of vegetables. One seller has a regular customer who comes every two weeks from Seattle, Washington, to stock up. Sweet potato greens are incredibly popular, but supply is limited. One shopper showed up at 5 AM to get in line, but others had gotten there even earlier. By the time she got to the front of the line, the greens were gone. Next time, she says, she'll get there at 3 AM.

Morris Gbolo immigrated from Liberia in 2002, trying to escape a civil war in West Africa. A farmer by trade, he found a natural fit in starting a New Jersey business that focuses on raising and selling African food. He's got a ready customer base of African immigrants, who welcome having a local source of food that saves them from the exorbitant prices of imported food. "I want to help feed people," Gbolo said in a 2015 interview with "Feet in 2 Worlds," a public radio program focusing on immigrants. "We're African, we love our native food."

In the Kitchen

Back at home with their bags of groceries, immigrants grappled with more changes. In many African countries, cooking a meal can be an all-day—or multiday—project, and it's almost always the women who do it. To Westerners, that may seem like an outdated attitude, but it makes sense in traditional African culture, where men typically spent most of their time away from home (and still do). Men expected their wives, sisters, or daughters to do the cooking, and it was a source of pride for women to do so. This arrangement changed somewhat with immigrants, because, at least at first, most of them were men. If they wanted food, they had to

In African cultures, women are expected to do most of the cooking, but immigrants find that they have to change some of these ways.

TVs for Food

For Nigerian immigrants who moved to Belgium several decades ago, it was the cold that struck them first. The climate in this Northern European country was far chillier than they were used to. Not surprisingly, many of the foods that grew well in the tropics of Nigeria were unheard of here. Every so often, though, these immigrants would catch a break. A Nigerian ship would arrive at one of the country's ports, loaded with food from home. Although most immigrants didn't have much money, they found a solution. They collected used appliances and electronics from the native Belgians—who were happy to unload their broken TVs and refrigerators—and then traded them as scrap to the Nigerian sailors. In return, they received new supplies of yams, dried fish and vegetables, and *egusi* (squash seeds).

either eat out or cook it themselves—neither of which was a common approach in most African cultures.

Dakpa Zady, who relates his story in the book *Breaking Bread: Recipes and Stories from Immigrant Kitchens*, immigrated to Boston, Massachusetts, from Côte d'Ivoire along with several other men. None of them knew how to cook—the women in their lives had always taken care of that. They got hungry soon enough, though, and they had to start somewhere, so they tackled a basic: rice. Next they moved on to sauces, which brought mixed success. The finished product always seemed to have too much salt or none at all. Then there was the problem of timing: they'd set the pot to **simmer** on the stove and forget all about it—until the smoke alarms started going off.

Zady also had to get used to the variety—and amount—of food in America. Looking at a pot of chicken with multiple legs and wings, "You'd think, Wow! How can this be? Back home there are certain parts of the chicken you don't even know about, because you've never had them. Someone else eats those—the good parts." Now Zady is an accomplished cook, something his family has a hard time believing. "When I tell them back home that I cook every day, they think I'm joking."

Making New Rules

Frustrations are part of an immigrant's daily diet—but so are some unexpected freedoms. Immigrants can take their food traditions with them, but leave behind the **taboos**. Nsedu Onyile, a woman from Nigeria, recounted her experiences as an immigrant in a 1995 *Washington Post* column—including her first taste of a goat's head. "Where I come from, the women fix and serve it on a big platter but only the men are entitled to eat it," she wrote. "As a child, I fantasized about the taste of the goat head and could not wait for an opportunity to eat one. Now, in a total declaration of independence, I buy goat from the slaughterhouse, fix the head first, and sit down to catch up on missed years."

In this park in Brazil, four statues in a small lake were put up to represent gods from the Candomblé religion.

Celebrations

As with any culture, holidays and celebrations are prime time for fancy dishes and family favorites. Due to Africa's size and diverse history, people from African countries practice a number of religions, primarily Islam and Christianity. There are also areas where the people still practice traditional tribal religions.

African immigrants sometimes brought their religions with them, sometimes adopted religions that were more common in their destination country, and sometimes combined both. In Brazil, for example, some people practice a religion called Candomblé. It combines practices found in traditional African tribal religions with elements of the Catholic religion that African slaves were introduced to in Central and South America. For many years it was dismissed by nonpractitioners as "witchcraft," but now it is more accepted. During the rituals of Candomblé, it's important that one particular food make an appearance—*acaçá*. The ingredients of acaçá are simple—a mush of ground corn wrapped in a banana leaf—but it must be prepared according to exact standards. Candomblé priests traditionally use **mortars and pestles** to grind the corn, and then carefully wrap the mush in a banana leaf to symbolize the creation of another body or being.

The best-known holidays have been around for centuries, but one that is celebrated primarily by African Americans is only about 50 years old. Kwanzaa was created in 1966 by Maulana Karenga, an activist and African studies scholar, who later became a professor. The year before, a bitter and violent race riot tore apart the neighborhood of Watts in South Los Angeles. To help with the healing, Karenga created Kwanzaa as a

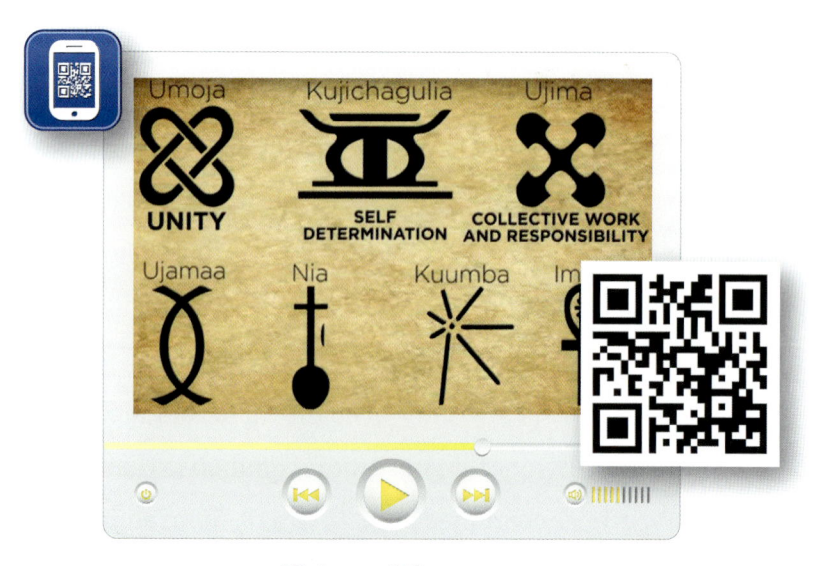

History of Kwanzaa

way to bring African Americans together to celebrate their heritage and to reconnect with values that were important in African communities. The holiday lasts a week, with each day devoted to a particular value or principle, such as unity, cooperation, and purpose. The word "Kwanzaa" comes from a Swahili phrase that means "first fruits," and Karenga designed the celebration using elements of harvest feasts found in traditional African cultures. Authentic African foods, as well as African American soul food standards, are often on the menu at the *karamu*, a feast held on Kwanzaa's sixth day.

Text-Dependent Questions:

1. What are two African vegetables that are popular at farmers' markets?
2. What was one way Nigerian immigrants in Belgium got food from Africa?
3. How did the religion of Candomblé arise from the slave trade?

Research Project:

Kwanzaa began as a holiday in the United States. Find out more about how it's spread throughout the world.

SECOND COURSE

Although many Africans today use modern kitchen appliances—refrigerators, stoves, ovens—many of their dishes developed when conditions were more primitive. With nothing more than a large iron pot, a long wooden spoon, and a tripod set up over an open fire, for centuries African cooks have created meals that are simple, economical—and delicious.

> The one-pot meal is common throughout most of Africa, and for good reason: Cooks can toss in a variety of vegetables, add whatever meat might be available, cook for a few hours, and it's ready to go. This simple style of eating is perfectly suited to the African lifestyle. A slow cooking process gives women (who do most of the cooking) time to take care of other chores while the stew is simmering. A single pot means there's only one dish to keep track of (and less to clean up afterward!). And there's a built-in versatility with a vegetable stew or medley of meat and beans, since they're easy to adapt to whatever happens to be available.

Although there's a lot of overlap in the raw ingredients available throughout Africa—from corn and coconuts to peanuts and plantains—each region of the continent does have its own specialties. In West Africa, for example, Jollof *rice is a beloved dish. The exact preparation varies according to the region—the Senegalese have one version, the Ghanians another, and the Nigerians still another take on this classic. Basically, a tomato base is bulked up with other vegetables, like bell peppers and onions, and then seasoned with the cook's choice of spices like curry, hot peppers, thyme, or ginger. It's all left to simmer for a while, and then mixed in with long-grain rice. The national dish of Senegal,* thieboudienne, *is a sumptuous stew that combines fish with a base that resembles Jollof rice—but don't try to convince people they're the same!*

SECOND COURSE

Wat, the national dish of Ethiopia, is a perfect example of how Ethiopians think it's important to take the time to cook something properly. It takes hours—or sometimes days—to make this signature meal, and there are often many pairs of hands at work. The dish starts with a base of onions sauteed in oil. Next comes berbere, a complex—and spicy!—blend of freshly ground seasonings that typically includes hot peppers, garlic, ginger, cardamom, coriander, allspice, and more. *Doro wat* uses chicken and hardboiled eggs, while *yebeg wat* is made with lamb. It's all scooped up with pieces of injera bread.

Meat isn't always readily available throughout all of Africa, but it's a big part of the cuisine in South Africa. Bobotie uses ground beef seasoned with breyani spices—another distinctive blend of spices that features cardamom, coriander, anise, fennel, bay leaves, and cinnamon. The meat is mixed with bread cubes soaked in milk; apples and jam are added to give the whole thing a bit of sweetness, and then it's all baked in an egg custard.

4

Reaching Back

Even just a few decades ago, it was much more difficult than it is now to stay in touch with people living far away. There was no email, no social media, no inexpensive ways to talk via Internet video. It took several days (or weeks) for a letter to cross the ocean, and it wasn't unusual for mail to go missing in poorer, developing countries with unreliable postal services. Meanwhile, telephones were limited to land lines, and even a short international call could be very expensive. That's assuming that someone in Africa even had a telephone—many did not!

Digging Up Their Roots

Sometimes, though, it's not a phone call or an email with someone thousands of miles away that immigrants use to reconnect with their homeland. Instead,

Words to Understand

cultivates grows, raises as food
mushrooming growing very quickly
staples key parts of a diet, whether ingredients or important dishes

Cell phones and email have solved most of the communications problems between African American families and their relatives back in Africa.

it's a conversation with someone who's right next door.

Alicia Ama comes from a family of African immigrants. Her grandparents were originally from Togo, but then moved across the country's western border to Ghana. Ama herself was born in Britain. In a 2016 interview with Hona Africa, a YouTube channel, Ama explains that as a second-generation immigrant, "Food is definitely my way of connecting with my history, my family, and learning about the culture. Typical African

Write It Down

You might be able to make mac and cheese without a recipe (especially if it comes in a box!), but if you tackle something more complicated, chances are you head straight for a cookbook to get a recipe. In many African cultures, however, women scoff at relying on a recipe. There, the mark of a good cook is someone who can produce a meal from scratch, using knowledge that's been passed down by word of mouth. That's starting to change, though. Especially for African immigrants, who are separated from the daily customs of their home countries, a little outside help is appreciated.

Cookbooks can also be a way to revive dishes that are in danger of being forgotten. In the 1970s, the government of South Africa declared a region called District Six to be only for white residents. Thousands of people were forced out of their homes. Years later, when they began to reconnect, they decided to publish a cookbook of dishes they remembered from their childhoods. The book is a mix of recipes, cooking tips, and stories from their youth.

parents are not really that forthcoming when it comes to talking about back home. You can ask them a question and they give you the shortest, most concise answer. But when I talk about food, that's a different story. My mum comes alive when I'm asking her, 'Mum, what did you used to eat when you were a kid? What did grandma used to make?' It was definitely a tool for a kid who was not able to connect fully with their African heritage or their Britishness."

Now, Ama runs a business cooking and selling traditional Ghanian and other West African foods in London. Asked to describe Ghanian food, she answers, "Filling, flavorful, and made with time and love. I'd say that's what makes a Ghanian dish." Her favorite? Plantain. "It's like medicine. I never get sick of it, ever," she laughs. "I can't live in a place that is more than five minutes drive away from a place where I can buy plantain."

African Ambassadors

With a student visa in hand, Makda Harlow considered herself one of the lucky ones. She left her eastern Africa home of Eritrea in 1989, during the final years of the country's 30-year war of independence, and came to America. Then, after 15 years living in various places in the United States, she married and moved to London with her husband. Having lived away from Africa in two different countries—and on two continents—Harlow understood what it meant to be an immigrant. She also wanted to use her love of food to connect her adopted country to her homeland, so she and her husband started a restaurant.

Eritrea has no culture of street food—buying quick, easy-to-eat, familiar food from carts, food trucks, or casual markets. London, on the other hand, was chock full of tacos, chicken wings, and fries. "We developed a

Africans settling in China have learned to adapt their food to use with the flavors and ingredients available there.

menu of street food **staples**, but made them with the unusual flavors of Eritrean cooking," Harlow explains. "We wanted to challenge the cliché of African food—big stews bubbling away and bowls of rice—and show that there was more to it. We wanted to surprise people with the flavors." Now, their customers are a mix of African immigrants and native Britons.

In Ghangzhou, China, Ghanian immigrant Frank Millen, along with his Chinese wife, Jessica Luo, opened a restaurant and began serving food from Millen's native Ghana. It was a success, but customers wanted even more variety, so the restaurant began offering a Pan-African menu, with dishes from several regions in Africa. And soon it wasn't just Africans coming for dinner—it was the local Chinese. While the African way of eating is for families to share a single large meal, Millen and Luo recognized that their Chinese customers wanted to try a little of everything, so they put together a sampler with small portions of several different dishes.

It's still a hurdle to navigate an entirely different culture, though. A Chinese restaurant reviewer gave the place a negative review, scorning the diners' custom of eating with their hands. Of course, that's traditional in Africa—and there were enough people who recognized that such a custom probably meant the place was authentic. When the review appeared in the newspaper, Millen reports that other Chinese diners were intrigued, and business picked up.

Here Comes Fonio

Fonio isn't new in Africa. This grain has been cultivated for centuries, and it's the basis of countless African dishes. Or it used to be, anyway. Senegalese chef Pierre Thiam notes that fonio is giving way to more familiar starches like rice, couscous, or quinoa—grains that were introduced by colonial powers and that Africans gradually came to prefer as "better" or more sophisticated. At his New York restaurant, Thiam offers dishes made with fonio—it's available, just expensive—and hopes to bring authentic African tastes to both African and non-African eaters. Ideally, he'd like to be part of an industry that **cultivates** fonio in Africa and then exports it, giving an economic boost to the regions that grow it. Others, however, are worried that a **mushrooming** fonio trade might go the way of coffee. The African coffee industry has historically exploited workers, and the same thing could happen if fonio became too popular.

New Traditions

Keeping food traditions alive in another country can be challenging. It's hard to find and afford the right ingredients, especially in countries that don't appreciate the subtle differences in African food. To a Western palate, the ingredients for sale in an African market may seem interchangeable, but to an immigrant, there are important distinctions—and not everything makes the cut. Cassava, for example, is a starchy root that's common throughout Africa. But not all cassava is the same. The kind people eat in the Congo is different from what Nigerians are used to. With limited food choices, immigrants may have to give up particular

Cassava is a versatile food, served in a wide variety of ways, depending on which country's recipes you are using.

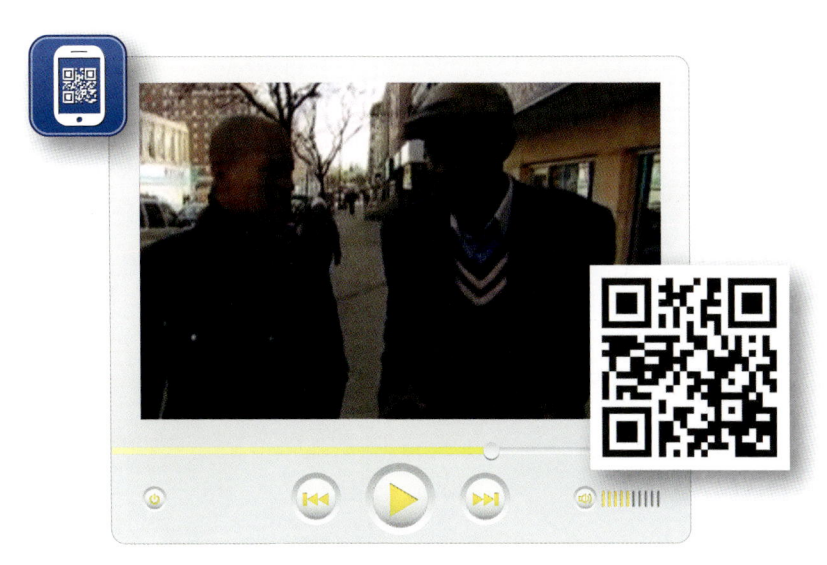

Bringing African food to New York City

foods or get used to preparing dishes with substitutes.

There's also the burden of feeling like an outsider. Many immigrant families change their eating habits to fit in more easily with their adopted society. They may eat out more often, for example, or turn to fast food and sweets instead of time-consuming homemade fare. Others work hard to serve traditional food when possible. After having children, Akinde Kodjo-Sanogo says, "I had to find a way to teach my children where I came from through my traditions, and especially the food we ate back in Africa. I cooked African dishes; every weekend we ate *attiéké* (cassava couscous) or *fufu* (made from plantain powder). It felt like a celebration for my children because these are their favorite foods."

Maintaining those culinary ties is certainly more work than grabbing a fast-food burger, but for many it's worth it. One young woman, interviewed for Maureen Duru's book *Diaspora, Food and Identity: Nigerian Migrants in Belgium* reported that even after she left home, she planned to eat her

The family table remains a vital way to connect the generations.

native food three times a week. "I also will expect any future partner to eat Nigerian food," she added. "How can you say you love a Nigerian girl but you don't like her food?"

Fortunately, that will probably be one of the future couple's easier things to get through, since Africans have a varied cuisine that's won over the taste buds of people around the world. Like all immigrants, Africans have faced challenges—and will continue to—as they resettle in new places. They will struggle to find the right balance between fitting in and remaining separate. Slowly, they will transform their new home even as it transforms them. Through it all, they can always gather to share a community meal, one where there's plenty to go around, and all are welcome. One where it doesn't matter where someone came from—just that they're together now.

Text-Dependent Questions:

1. What is Alicia Ama's favorite food?

2. How did Makda Harlow decide to introduce Eritrean cuisine in London?

3. After settling in the United States, what traditional African dishes did Akinde Kodjo-Sanogo make for her children?

Research Project:

Plan your own African feast. Make a guest list, decide what dishes you want to make, and start finding recipes. Where will you buy the ingredients? If you can't find some, what substitutes can you use?

DESSERT

Tell an African child that there's no dessert unless she eats dinner, and you might just get a blank stare. Dessert isn't part of most traditional African cuisine—and especially not the super sweet, heavy, and rich desserts that are part of American and European cooking. Nor do Africans worry too much about the after-dinner timing. When they do crave something sweet, they'll indulge no matter what the time of day. Fried sweet balls—like doughnut holes—turn up in different variations all over Africa, and fresh fruit is always a good choice. For a special treat in Kenya, people might just add some raisins to vermicelli (very thin pasta).

Peanuts are a popular crop throughout Africa, and as any fan of peanut butter knows, they're particularly good when helped along with a little sugar. In West Africa, ground peanuts, rice flour, and sugar are pressed together into fudge-like squares called kanyah. *A similar East African version,* kashata, *(pictured at right) adds in coconut as well.*

Dessert 59

Think oatmeal with a twist: caakiri or thiakry *(top) is a type of porridge or pudding made from a grain such as millet, maize, or couscous. Diners can then add milk, cream, yogurt, or buttermilk, plus sugar, nutmeg, and dried fruit, to make a tasty dessert. A similar dish is* ngalakh *(bottom) which substitutes peanut butter and* bouye *(fruit from the baobab tree) for cream and sugar.*

Connecting Cultures Through Family and Food

Some areas in Africa reflect more European influences. That has shown up in their food preferences at home—and in what they took with them when they emigrated to other countries. In South Africa, milk, eggs, sugar, and flour are mixed together and baked in a pastry shell to make melktert. That's "milk tart" in Afrikaans, a language spoken in several countries in southern Africa. The language comes from the Dutch, and so does this custard pie dessert.

RECIPE

Attiéké
This dish, popular in Cote d'Ivoire and Benin, starts with cassava, which is peeled, grated, and then fermented. The attiéké can be prepared fresh, but it's also possible to buy it frozen.

Ingredients:
  1 kg (2.2 pounds) frozen attiéké (cassava)
  ½ pound chicken
  olive oil
  2 large tomatoes
  2 large onions
  Salt, pepper, and other seasonings to taste

Preparation:
Defrost the attiéké for one hour and break into pieces. Add a ¼ cup of water and microwave for four minutes or until fully thawed.

Stir, add a teaspoon of salt, and let it cool.

Cut chicken into bite-size pieces and season to taste. Sauté in olive oil on medium-high heat until thoroughly cooked (about 15 minutes).

Cut tomatoes and onions into two-inch pieces, and toss with olive oil, salt, pepper, and other seasonings. Preheat oven to 425°F and roast for 20 minutes.

Stir chicken, tomatoes, and onions into prepared attiéké. Enjoy!

Find Out More

Books

Asgedom, Mawi. *Of Beetles and Angels: A Boy's Remarkable Journey from a Refugee Camp to Harvard.* New York: Little, Brown Books for Young Readers, 2002.

Bowen, Richard A. *The African Americans.* Broomall, PA: Mason Crest, 2008.

Montgomery, Bertha Vining, and Constance Nabwire. *Cooking the West African Way.* Minneapolis, MN: Lerner Publications, 2002. (Also check out other titles in this series, *Cooking the East African Way, Cooking the South African Way*, and *Cooking the North African Way*.)

Worth, Richard. *Africans in America.* New York, NY: Facts on File, 2004.

Websites

http://www.pbs.org/wnet/african-americans-many-rivers-to-cross/history/on-african-american-migrations/
Learn more about the history of African American immigration, from the slave trade through modern migrations.

http://www.loc.gov/teachers/classroommaterials/presentationsandactivities/presentations/immigration/alt/african.html
African immigrants have had a profound effect on American culture. Read about their history and contributions here.

https://www.africaguide.com/culture/cooking.htm
Check out some of the basic ingredients and spices used in African cooking, then click on the links to explore recipes from different regions of Africa.

Series Glossary of Key Terms

acclimate to get used to something

assimilate become part of a different society, country, or group

bigotry treating the members of a racial or ethnic group with hatred and intolerance

culinary having to do with the preparing of food

diaspora a group of people who live outside the area in which they had lived for a long time or in which their ancestors lived

emigrate leave one's home country to live in another country

exodus a mass departure of people from one place to another

first-generation American someone born in the United States whose parents were foreign born

immigrants those who enter another country intending to stay permanently

naturalize to gain citizenship, with all its rights and privileges

oppression a system of forcing people to follow rules or a system that restricts freedoms

presentation in this series, the style in which food is plated and served

Index

acacá, 42
Algerian immigrants, 14
appetizers, 20-21
art, 27
black pride, 27-28
Candomblé, 41-42
celebrations, 41-43
Chibinda Ilunga, 10
civil rights, 28
Civil Rights Act, 15
Civil War, 12-13, 22, 26
colonial rule, 13-14
commodities, 10
cookbooks, 27
cooking, 38, 40
cuisine, 24-26, 30-33
cultural barriers, 29
dance, 27
desserts, 58-61
discrimination, 28-29
economic depressions, 17-18
European nations, 17, 28
fonio, 53
food traditions, 54-57
French, 16
Ghanaian food, 51
grocery stores, 34-37
Harlem Renaissance, 27
history, 6-8, 10
holidays, 41-43
hospitality, 25
jobs, 18, 27, 30
Kwanzaa, 42-43
language, 16, 29
laws, 15-16
main courses, 32-33
markets, 37
middle passage, 10, 13
modern migrations, 17
mortars, 42
music, 27, 29
networking, 30
New York, 27
pesties, 42
prejudices, 15
race riots, 42
reconnecting, 48, 50-51
Refugee Act, 16
religions, 41
restaurants, 30, 52-53
second courses, 44-47
slave cooks, 25
slave trade, 10-12
slaves, 22, 24, 26
soul food, 28, 43
South Africa, 13
street food, 51-52
students, 15
sub-Saharan Africa, 17
taboos, 40
trading, 39
trans-Atlantic trade, 10
triangle trade, 10
white masters, 22, 24-25
workers, 18

Photo Credits

Alamy Stock: Interfoto 13; Lanmas 22; Alan Wilson 36. AP Images: Imaginechina 52. Dreamstime.com: Adou Innocent Kouadio 7, Nagg1979 16, MBI 17, Paul Brighton 19, Xalanx 20, Yulilia Kononenko 21T, Kurapy11 21B, Innose 25, Mujib Waziri 32, Alexander Mychko 33T, Nastya22 33B, Joan Egert 35, Robert Lerich 39, Antoni Halim 40, fultonsphoto 44, Ppy2010ha 45, Dndavis 49, Valeria Gilardi 53, Luiz Ribiero 54, MBI 56, Sohadiszno 58, Alexander Mychko 59T, Toscawhi 60. NARA: 15. Newscom: Christian Murdock/MCT 29; Bob Fila/KRT 30. Shutterstock: Fedor Salivanov 9, vm2002 24, Sarine Arslanian 38. Wikimedia CC: Wellcome Trust 11; 12; Diego Grandi 41; 59B; Zak Le Messenger 61.

Author Bio

Diane Bailey has written more than 50 nonfiction books for kids and teens, on topics ranging from science to sports to celebrities. She also works as a freelance editor, helping authors who write novels for children and young adults. Diane has two sons and two dogs, and lives in Kansas.